There Are No Wrong Answers

A Book of Quizzes

There Are No Wrong Answers

A Book of Quizzes

By Emma Sector

ALADDIN
New York   London   Toronto   Sydney   New Delhi

ALADDIN

An imprint of Simon & Schuster Children's Publishing Division

1230 Avenue of the Americas, New York, New York 10020

First Aladdin paperback edition May 2016

Text copyright © 2016 by Emma Sector

Illustrations copyright © 2016 by Allie Smith

For information about special discounts for bulk purchases, please contact Simon & Schuster Special Sales at 1-866-506-1949 or business@simonandschuster.com.

The Simon & Schuster Speakers Bureau can bring authors to your live event. For more information or to book an event contact the Simon & Schuster Speakers Bureau at 1-866-248-3049 or visit our website at www.simonspeakers.com.

Cover designed by Gail Ghezzi and Steve Scott

Interior designed by Steve Scott

The text of this book was set in ITC American Typewriter.

Manufactured in the United States of America 0416 OFF

2 4 6 8 10 9 7 5 3 1

Library of Congress Control Number 2015940157

ISBN 978-1-4814-5932-7 (pbk)

ISBN 978-1-4814-5933-4 (eBook)

Contents

To Mom and Dad.
You guys are great!

And to Abby Anastas—
thanks for all the help!

←—# CHAPTER #—→

1

Let's Party!

What should the theme of your birthday party be?

What kind of birthday cake are you?

What kind of partygoer are you?

What famous inventor should you invite
to your birthday party?

What book-inspired gift should you give

······················· [insert name here] ·······················

for their birthday?

1

What should the theme of your birthday party be?

1. Choose a print.

    A. flowers

    B. stripes

    C. plaid

    D. splatter paint

2. Time of day you want your party?

    A. midmorning

    B. afternoon

    C. evening

    D. all day

3. Choose a dessert.

    A. cupcakes

    B. mud cups (cups of chocolate pudding, crushed Oreos, and gummy worms)

    C. regular cake

    D. ice cream cake

4. Choose a decoration.

A. glitter

B. banners with your name on them

C. a set dining room table, complete with candles and a tablecloth

D. confetti

5. Choose a party outfit.

A. a really fancy outfit

B. comfy shorts and a T-shirt

C. cool shirt and pants/skirt

D. whatever, you'll probably stain it anyway

6. Choose a birthday crown.

A. a tiara

B. the classic gold-paper crown

C. not into crowns, but a cool hat would be nice

D. a crown made out of flowers

7. Choose a bag for your party favors.

A. a drawstring pouch

B. a movie popcorn bucket

C. Chinese takeout container

D. brown paper bags that you have custom designed for each guest

Results!

Mostly As: Marie Antoinette Tea Party

Throw a party fit for Marie Antoinette! The French queen is best known for her over-the-top, glamorous life style. Turn your living room or backyard into a decadent tea parlor by piling tables with tiny cupcakes and cookies. Put lots of glitter, floral patterns, and doilies everywhere. You can even ask your guests to dress up for the occasion and give everyone a fan and white gloves when they walk in.

Mostly Bs: World Cup Party

Re-create the World Cup! Divide everyone into teams of five and have a big soccer tournament. Make a T-shirt decorating station on the sidelines for the teams that aren't playing. If the party is indoors, clear a space inside and play floor soccer with an inflatable beach ball. Give out medals and have a celebratory feast at the end.

Mostly Cs: Murder Mystery Dinner Party

Ask someone (not a guest) to play the part of the butler for the night to deliver clues. Create a murder mystery to solve (look online for ideas), and give clues throughout the night. Everyone can dress up like a famous detective. (Some ideas: Sherlock Holmes, Nancy Drew, Hardy Boys, Timmy Failure, Scooby-Doo, Harriet the Spy.)

Mostly Ds: Art Party

Inspire your guests with a painting party! Put lots of paints, pencils, and brushes in the middle of a table. Give everyone a pre-stretched canvas (you can get them at any craft store), and hang up reproductions of your favorite paintings around the room for inspiration. Put out bowls of popcorn so you can snack while you work. At the end of the party, replace all the art examples around the room with your masterpieces. End the party with a gallery opening with drinks and finger foods.

What kind of
birthday cake are you?

1. When you go out for ice cream . . .

    A. you always get the same flavor

    B. you're all about combining different flavors
       in one cup

    C. you rotate between a few different flavors

    D. every time you get a different flavor

2. Favorite holiday?

    A. Thanksgiving

    B. Fourth of July

    C. your birthday

    D. New Year's Eve

3. Choose a pattern to paint your nails.

    A. polka dots

    B. a geometric pattern with three colors

    C. splatter-paint nails

    D. a different tiny face for each nail

4. Which of the following do you want for breakfast?

A. pancakes and maple syrup

B. french toast with strawberries and whipped cream

C. cinnamon rolls with rainbow sprinkles

D. chocolate-chip-and-marshmallow waffles

5. If you were an animal, what animal would you be?

A. a dog

B. a penguin

C. a monkey

D. a zebra

Results!

Mostly As: Chocolate Cake

You love the simple things in life and always make people feel right at home.

Mostly Bs: Ice Cream Cake

You are a party favorite. You love hanging with friends; the more the merrier!

Mostly Cs: Rainbow Cake

You're super fun and original. You love cracking people up with a joke or a crazy outfit.

Mostly Ds: A Platter of Many Cupcakes

You love new experiences and trying new things. Making decisions is always hard, because everything always sounds good!

What kind of partygoer are you?

1. Which TV competition would you enter?

A. *Shark Tank*

B. *Dancing with the Stars*

C. *America's Funniest Home Videos*

D. *Project Runway*

2. Favorite weekend activity?

A. hanging out with friends

B. going to play or dance practice

C. playing or watching sports

D. reading

3. Favorite dance move?

A. the twist (basically just twisting your body side to side)

B. no moves, you just go with the music

C. the robot

D. the pogo (jumping up and down like you're on a pogo stick)

4. Pick a party to attend.

   A. sleepover party

   B. dance party

   C. water balloon fight party

   D. picnic party

5. What's a good birthday gift to give a friend?

   A. a board game

   B. an iTunes gift card (with some suggestions)

   C. a funny T-shirt

   D. homemade cupcakes

Results!

Mostly As: The Conversationalist

You're really good at finding things to talk about. You're full of weird facts and are really good at telling a story. It doesn't take long for a stranger to become your best friend!

Mostly Bs: The Dance Machine

Parties are for dancing, you always say. You're the first one to put on the music and get everyone out on the dance floor.

Mostly Cs: The Party Animal

You're always telling jokes and having fun at a party. If something out of the ordinary is happening, it's definitely because of you.

Mostly Ds: The Wallflower

You prefer to lie low at a party. You can always be found having longer conversations with good friends rather than bopping around from conversation to conversation.

What famous inventor from the past should you invite to your birthday party?

1. What would you like to see out your window?

A. a spaceship flying through the sky

B. a traveling circus coming into town

C. your friends carrying a giant cake

D. a hot-air balloon about to make a landing on the ground below you

2. Favorite subject in school?

A. science

B. How could you choose? You love something about all of them!

C. math

D. art class

3. Dream job?

A. astronaut

B. writer for *National Geographic*

C. talk show host

D. ice cream flavor inventor

4. What's the best way to pass the time on a long car ride?

　　A. taking pictures of cool things you pass

　　B. looking out the window and observing the world around you

　　C. solving riddles

　　D. Mad Libs

5. How do you solve a problem?

　　A. If at first you don't succeed, try, try again!

　　B. You think about it from every perspective and then make a decision.

　　C. Talk it over with your best friend.

　　D. Draw it on paper so you can really visualize the problem.

Results!

Mostly As: Barbara Askins

Barbara Askins invented a way to develop photos from space so that we could actually see what the picture was of. All those crazy photos of Earth? That's because of Barbara! She was a teacher first and then started working for NASA. Like Barbara, you never give up on your dreams. She could give you great advice and take some truly stellar pictures at your party.

Mostly Bs: Benjamin Franklin

Benjamin Franklin invented bifocals, swimming fins, a lightning rod, and tons more! Like you, he had an appetite for learning. He taught himself so much that he earned honorary degrees from Harvard *and*

Yale. Just like Ben, you love to discover new things. You guys would have a lot of fun, chatting about how things work, and he would bring a super-unique birthday present.

Mostly Cs: Alexander Graham Bell

Alexander Graham Bell is best known for inventing the telephone. Just like Alexander, you love to solve problems. When you get an idea in your head, you can't wait to see it through. You and Alexander could talk about your ideas over cake and ice cream.

Mostly Ds: Leonardo da Vinci

Though he's most famous for his painting *Mona Lisa*, Leonardo da Vinci invented the first scuba suit, a traveling bridge (it could be packed up to take with you), and a robot. He also designed the first airplane and parachute, but they would not be made until centuries after he died. Like Leonardo, you love to think up crazy inventions. You're more of a thinker than an experimenter, though. It's why art is so appealing to you. You can create what your mind envisions with the stroke of a paintbrush. Leo would be a really fun party guest. He could tell everyone what Mona Lisa was thinking about!

What book-inspired gift should you give .... (insert name here) for their birthday?

1. What kind of shoes do they like to wear?

    A. sneakers

    B. boots

    C. sandals

    D. no shoes unless they have to

2. What's their favorite season?

    A. spring

    B. fall

    C. winter

    D. summer

3. If they were a superhero, they would be . . .

    A. Batman

    B. the Hulk

    C. Wonder Woman

    D. Spider-Man

4. What type of movies do they like best?

    A. action

    B. horror

    C. fantasy

    D. comedy

5. If they lived under the sea, they would be . . .

    A. a jellyfish

    B. a shark

    C. a mermaid

    D. a blowfish

Results!

Mostly As:
Hatchet by Gary Paulsen

For the adventurer. Give them a copy of this great American adventure story with a world map, a compass, a notebook, and a pen. Now they can go anywhere and can record their own adventures.

Mostly Bs:
Scary Stories to Tell in the Dark by Alvin Schwartz

For your Halloween-obsessed friend. They love anything scary, so give them the collection of short stories that has scared for decades. Combine with newspaper strips, flour, balloons, and a set of paints. They now have a scary-mask-making kit!

Mostly Cs:
Alice in Wonderland by Lewis Carroll

For the dreamer. Give them a copy of this classic story, a box of tea, a teacup, a tin of homemade cookies, and a journal. All the materials for a perfect afternoon of daydreaming.

Mostly Ds:
Holes by Louis Sachar

For the unintentional troublemaker. Like the main character of this classic story, your friend has their heart in the right place but always seems to get into trouble somehow. They love adventure, so throw a surprise party with an elaborate scavenger hunt with all your friends.

❦ CHAPTER ❦

2

All About Fashion

What is your signature jacket?

What is your must-have accessory?

What famous fashion designer
is your kindred spirit?

What is your spirit print?

What era in American fashion
should inspire your next outfit?

What is your signature jacket?

1. Which is your favorite of Grimm's fairy tales?

    A. Little Red Riding Hood

    B. Hansel and Gretel

    C. Cinderella

    D. Snow White

2. Pick a hat.

    A. party hat

    B. baseball cap

    C. top hat

    D. snow hat

3. What type of winter activity do you like best?

    A. ice-skating

    B. making a snow fort

    C. hanging inside by the fire

    D. snowball fights

4. Pick a pair of pants.

A. pants with a fun pattern

B. overalls

C. skinny jeans

D. loose jeans with paint on them

5. Which animal would you like to be?

A. a bunny

B. a dog

C. a horse

D. a tiger

Results!

Mostly As: Cape

You should have a jacket fit for Cinderella's court! This unique jacket will have you looking like you walked right out of a fairy tale.

Mostly Bs: Jean Jacket

You are casual cool, and your style should be too. Your signature coat is the classic jean jacket. It goes with everything, and it's always in style.

Mostly Cs: Trench Coat

You are classy and stylish and are always on top of trends. You deserve a coat that will always look as fabulous as you do.

Mostly Ds: Motorcycle Jacket

You love to take risks and have adventures! Like you, this coat is very fun and fits in anywhere.

What is your must-have accessory?

1. How do you like to wear your hair?

   A. Curled. It takes a lot of effort, but it looks the best.

   B. Up. You hate when your hair's in your face.

   C. dyed crazy colors

   D. just down, nothing special

2. What's your favorite way to sit?

   A. crisscross applesauce on the floor

   B. relaxed in an armchair

   C. How to choose? Really depends on the circumstance.

   D. curled up on the couch under a blanket

3. Which superpower would you want most?

   A. to fly

   B. to be invisible

   C. to shoot laser beams from your eyes

   D. to read people's minds

4. If you had a garden filled with only one type of plant, what plant would you choose?

A. lemon trees

B. apple trees

C. tulips in every color

D. sunflowers

5. If you won the lottery, you would . . .

A. buy a boat and sail around the world

B. put it in the bank for when you need it

C. buy a bunch of new clothes

D. throw a huge party for all your friends

Results!

Mostly As: Costume Jewelry

Whether it's dangling earrings, a necklace, or a giant ring, your must-have accessory is big, bold, and fun jewelry. You like to make a statement, so your accessory should too.

Mostly Bs: A Watch

Your must-have accessory is just as practical as you are. And, as you know, practical does *not* mean boring. It can be oversize, neon, bejeweled. . . . The options are endless.

Mostly Cs: Piled Necklaces

You have a hard time making decisions. Pile different necklaces together, and then you don't have to choose just one thing. Each necklace can represent something that's special to you.

Mostly Ds: Colorful Patterned Socks

You like to be comfortable most of all. Roll up your pants a little to show off your patterned socks for an extra pop of color.

What famous fashion designer is your kindred spirit?

1. In what tree would you like your tree house?

A. an apple tree in an orchard where all your friends have tree houses too

B. a weeping willow next to a pond, where you have a rowboat that you row through the branches that hang down to the water

C. a palm tree on the beach, with a slide that goes into the ocean

D. a maple tree with a magical tap that puts syrup on your pancakes

2. Would you rather . . .

A. go swimming in the rain

B. watch the clouds float by from your bedroom window

C. go to the beach when it's snowing

D. hike a mountain in the fog

3. Which material would you like a pair of gloves made out of?

A. a cloud

B. rose petals

C. a painting

D. the plastic packing material that's fun to pop

4. How would you like to watch the sunset?

A. from a parachute as you drop down to a field of flowers beneath you

B. from a garden on the rooftop of a very tall building in a big city

C. from the top of a mountain with a magical-looking mist floating below you

D. through the window of a car as you speed toward a place you've never been to before

5. Which would you like to travel in?

A. a convertible

B. a sailboat

C. a school bus painted crazy colors

D. a spaceship

Results!

Mostly As: Coco Chanel

Coco is known for revolutionizing women's fashion by making it comfortable and easy to move in. Like Coco, you are a risk taker. You would never let customs and preconceived notions hold you back from fun. You feel comfortable in your own skin and confident in your choices.

Mostly Bs: Christian Dior

You're romantic and whimsical. You love floral patterns and soft pinks. Embrace your inner dreamer! Christian Dior is known for his beautiful fabrics and dresses shaped like flowers. You see fashion as an art form and love to put together a beautiful outfit.

Mostly Cs: Vivienne Westwood

Vivienne Westwood shook up the fashion world when she brought punk fashions (dark eyeliner, plaids, and towering heels) into the mainstream. You think of life as one big adventure, and clothes should be fun, not serious.

Mostly Ds: Pierre Cardin

With metallic fabrics and weird shapes, Pierre Cardin's styles seem straight out of Star Wars. Like Pierre, you are not afraid of the unknown. You want to know what it's like to walk on the moon and when you'll be able to pick up your jet pack. You always look toward the future: that's where all the fun will be!

What is your spirit print?

1. If you joined the circus, what would you be?

A. an acrobat

B. the elephant handler

C. the ringleader

D. the leader of the band

2. If you lived in a world made of candy, what would your house be made of?

A. chocolate

B. candy canes

C. gingerbread

D. jelly beans

3. If you were famous, what would you be famous for?

A. singing

B. writing novels

C. having your own show, as a newscaster or talk show host

D. acting in movies

4. You just got some flowers. Where would you like to put them?

A. in your hair

B. a pretty bottle

C. a glass vase

D. in whatever's around; it's the flowers that matter

5. When procrastinating, you like to . . .

A. doodle

B. read

C. clean

D. talk to people

Results!

Mostly As: Leopard Print

Like the animal this print was modeled after, you are smart and strong. You have bold new ideas and like to stand out.

Mostly Bs: Stripes

You feel comfortable in many different situations, and you have no trouble making new friends because you can find something you have in common with everyone.

Mostly Cs: Block Colors

You like things to be clear; you're all about honesty and organization. You're good at making plans and sticking to them. When you get excited about something, there's no holding you back!

Mostly Ds: Polka Dots

You like to laugh and hang with your pals. You're the relaxed one, the one to remind everyone to take it easy when tensions are high.

What era in American fashion should inspire your next outfit?

1. Which class would you like to take?

A. dance

B. drama

C. guitar

D. crafting

2. Which object would you like for your room?

A. a secret room behind a bookshelf

B. a vanity (fancy table with mirrors) with big colorful bottles

C. a projector

D. a beanbag chair

3. Pick a fabric.

A. sequined

B. silk

C. denim

D. metallic

4. If you were in a production of *The Wizard of Oz*, you would want to play . . .

A. the Scarecrow

B. Dorothy

C. the Tin Man

D. the Wicked Witch of the West

5. Pick a shoe.

A. tap shoe

B. high heel

C. sneaker

D. tall boot

36

Results!

Mostly As: 1920s Flapper

It's the era of *The Great Gatsby*! Loose dresses with tassels, headbands with feathers. . . . The flapper was fun and inventive, just like you!

Mostly Bs: Hollywood Glamour of the 1930s

Think feather boas and silk dresses, dramatic makeup, and short silky hair. This is the fashion of the poised and, of course, glamorous. Perfect for a diva such as yourself.

Mostly Cs: 1950s Rock and Roll

Grease was set in this era. It was the time of poodle skirts with sneakers, rolled-up jeans with white T-shirts, and skirts with big belts. There was new music and new approaches to life.

Mostly Ds: 1970s Disco

Think flashy materials and dresses made to stand out in a crowd. The disco era was all about being yourself, no matter how weird!

CHAPTER

3

Time Travel

What invention should you bring back
from your travels into the future?

What ancient structure mystery
should you travel back in time to solve?

What extinct animal would be your perfect pet?

What author should you talk to over tea?

Which legendary queen from history are you?

What invention should you bring back from your travels into the future?

1. What's your favorite part about flying on a plane?

A. looking at the world from so high up and feeling close to the clouds

B. sitting back and relaxing and then, almost magically, arriving in an entirely different place

C. sitting next to someone you've never met before

D. It's always exciting, because you're either on your way somewhere new or on your way home.

2. Favorite thing to do at a carnival?

A. roller coaster

B. teacups

C. bumper cars

D. win prizes

3. Pick a chair.

A. a swing

B. a hammock

C. a couch

D. a counter stool (that spins)

4. What's your favorite kind of book?

A. fantasy

B. mystery

C. realistic fiction

D. cookbook

5. What do you want to do for your birthday?

A. go to an amusement park

B. go on a trip to the beach

C. have a big party and invite all your friends

D. go to a fancy dinner and order all your favorite foods

Results!

Mostly As: Jet Pack

You're an adventurer, and a jet pack will be the perfect way for you to get around. You can do figure eights in the air on your way to school!

Mostly Bs: A Self-Navigating Hovercraft

You love to relax and you love to travel. What's better than something that drives itself and is comfortable to lounge in?

Mostly Cs: A Robot Friend

You're all about meeting new people and making new friends. A robot will be a fun companion that will know tons of cool facts.

Mostly Ds: A Special Microwave That Will Make Any Food You Ask It To

You love to eat great food and try new things. This is the gadget that will literally keep on giving.

What ancient structure mystery should you travel back in time to solve?

1. Which would you like to be most?

    A. a professional athlete

    B. a witch

    C. a spy

    D. a journalist

2. Choose a geographic feature.

    A. river

    B. cove

    C. mountain

    D. oasis

3. Pick a detective's outfit.

    A. a trench coat and a fedora

    B. a casual outfit, such as a sweater and jeans

    C. whatever the locals are wearing; you have to blend in

    D. something comfortable

43

4. Which crime-solving character would you like to be?

A. Indiana Jones

B. Sherlock Holmes

C. Nancy Drew

D. Batman

5. What mythical city would you most like to visit?

A. El Dorado

B. Camelot

C. Atlantis

D. Mount Olympus

Results!

Mostly As: The Great Pyramid at Giza

We've all wondered how the pyramids were created without bulldozers and cement. You are known for your perseverance and persistence. You can withstand the hot sun and dry heat to find out how this pyramid was built. Don't forget to bring water!

Mostly Bs: Stonehenge

There are many speculations about how and why Stonehenge was created. This mystery is going to be solved by chatting with the locals, and you have a knack for getting people to talk. Be sure to take notes!

Mostly Cs: Machu Picchu

Incredibly, the structures of this ancient city have remained intact. Archeologists have figured a lot out from what the Incas left behind, but questions remain: Why so high up in the mountains? What members of Incan society lived there? You're great at blending in, so you will be the perfect person to solve this mystery.

Mostly Ds: Hanging Gardens of Babylon

These gardens are thought to have been unbelievably beautiful. Hundreds of different types of plants grew in an oasis and formed around intricate columns. No one has ever discovered traces of them, so it is suggested that they are simply a myth. You always have a clear head and are not influenced by others, so you will be able to get to the bottom of this mystery once and for all.

What extinct animal would be your perfect pet?

1. What would you like to do with your pet?

A. float and play in the ocean

B. play in the snow

C. play fetch

D. ride it around

2. Which food do you like the best?

A. sushi

B. salad

C. BLT (bacon, lettuce, and tomato sandwich)

D. veggie burger

3. What game would you rather play?

A. Marco Polo

B. snowball fight

C. red rover

D. hide-and-seek

4. If you were to befriend a mythical creature, which would you choose?

A. mermaid

B. Sasquatch

C. dragon

D. centaur

5. People would describe you as . . .

A. chill

B. friendly

C. athletic

D. unique

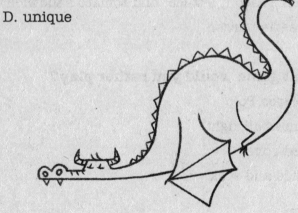

Results!

Mostly As: The Sea Cow (went extinct almost three hundred years ago)

The sea cow is a relative of the manatee and is one of the largest mammals that has ever existed. The sea cow is a very chill animal; it moves slowly and likes to float around the sea. You guys can swim long distances together; just take a nap on its back when you get tired.

Mostly Bs: Woolly Mammoth (went extinct four thousand years ago)

Like an elephant, the woolly mammoth is very large, with a big trunk. Scientists have studied fossils of mammoths' brains and learned that their behavior is also similar to that of elephants, which means they are very friendly and love to play. It would be like having a moving jungle gym. The mammoth's thick coat of fur would make it a great friend to have in the snow.

Mostly Cs: Eoraptor (went extinct over 230 million years ago)

This is one of the smallest known dinosaurs. An average Eoraptor didn't grow bigger than three feet. It would be kind of like having a dog but better because . . . well . . . it would be a mini *dinosuar*!

Mostly Ds: Quagga (extinct about 140 years ago)

With a zebra head and a horse behind, the quagga looked like a Dr. Seuss character. You guys would have many fun and strange travels together.

What author should you talk to over tea?

1. If you were an author, what would you write about?

A. friendships

B. kings and queens

C. silly things

D. scary things

2. Pick a famous character.

A. Cinderella

B. Robin Hood

C. Anne of Green Gables

D. Frankenstein

3. When do you feel most calm?

A. when you're taking a walk outside

B. when you're watching a movie

C. when you're reading

D. when you're writing

4. If you were a fine artist, what material would you use?

A. acrylics (regular paint)

B. marble

C. crayons

D. pencil

5. Favorite sky?

A. a sunrise in the spring

B. twilight, the moon just beginning to rise

C. the sunset in the summer

D. nighttime with a full moon

Results!

Mostly As: Jane Austen

You should visit Jane Austen on your travels back in time. You both have a sense of right and wrong, but you're optimistic that things will work out in the end.

Mostly Bs: William Shakespeare

You and Shakespeare could have some great chats about identity. You both like to understand characters and think about them critically.

Mostly Cs: Dr. Seuss, or Theodor Seuss Geisel

Like Dr. Seuss, you know that learning doesn't have to be serious. Sometimes the best lessons are learned when you're laughing. Be warned, you'll probably leave with a bellyache from the giggles, and a headache from all the things he made you think about.

Mostly Ds: Edgar Allan Poe

Before there was R. L. Stine or Ransom Riggs, there was Edgar Allan Poe. Even though he wrote in the mid-1800s, his stories are still relevant (and scary!) today. You guys would have a great time swapping ghost stories.

Which legendary queen from history are you?

1. Pick a character.

    A. Charlotte, from *Charlotte's Web*

    B. Dorothy, from *The Wizard of Oz*

    C. Eloise, from *Eloise*

    D. Willy Wonka, from *Charlie and the Chocolate Factory*

2. What is the most important thing to do as a leader?

    A. listen to your people's problems

    B. protect your people from outside forces

    C. make your country prosperous

    D. make sure everyone everyone has fair access to resources

3. Which job would you most like to have?

    A. lawyer

    B. firefighter

    C. architect

    D. president

4. Who would be your fictional archnemesis?

A. Voldemort

B. Loki

C. Captain Hook

D. Cruella de Vil

5. What annoys you most?

A. when people don't listen to you

B. when people underestimate you

C. when you can't get things done

D. when things are unfair

Results!

Mostly As: Liliuokalani, Hawaiian Queen, 1891–1893

Though Liliuokalani was queen for only a short time, she is still remembered as a fair and powerful leader. Above all, she wanted to free her country from overseas rule. She stood up to bigger and more powerful countries because it was what her people wanted. Like Liliuokalani, you will always do the right thing, even if it's not the easiest.

Mostly Bs: Rani of Jhansi, Queen of the Jhansi State (north-central part of India), mid-nineteenth century

Rani of Jhansi is known as a fierce warrior who protected her country to the end of her life. She was highly educated and invented great battle strategies when fighting against invaders. She was known to ride into battle and fight alongside her army. Like Rani, you are fearless and confident. You don't need anyone to fight your battles because you can do it yourself.

Mostly Cs: Hatshepsut, Egyptian Pharaoh, 1479–1458 BC

Hatshepsut is regarded as one of the most successful pharaohs of ancient Egypt. Her reign was peaceful and prosperous. She expanded trade routes extensively and may have been the first person to transport trees long distances by using baskets. She was able to build many new temples, statues, and buildings. Like Hatshepsut, you make things happen. You have big ideas and know what it takes to make them a reality.

Mostly Ds: Wu Zetian, Chinese Empress in Tang Dynasty China, 655–683 AD

Empress Wu is the only female emperor in Chinese history. She made political leaders take exams, not just rely on connections. She challenged beliefs about women by having scholars write biographies of powerful women. Like Empress Wu, you believe in fairness. You will always fight for people to be given equal opportunities.

CHAPTER
4

DIY Decorating for Your Bedroom

* Remember to check with your parents before taking on any of these projects!

What kind of plant should you grow in your room?

What DIY lamp best suits your personality?

How should you decorate your walls?

What kind of wind chime should you make to hang from your window?

What is the perfect theme for your bedroom?

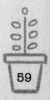

What kind of plant should you grow in your room?

1. Have you ever taken care of a plant before?

A. yes, with help from others

B. nope, but you're confident that your thumb is green

C. yes, with great success

D. yes, but never successfully

2. What's the light situation in your room?

A. not a ton of light, but there's some

B. it's always super sunny

C. very little light

D. sunny for most of the day

3. Temperature of your room?

A. it's a comfortable temperature

B. it gets pretty hot

C. cool

D. kinda warm

4. Do you have a lot of room for a plant?

    A. you have a corner you can give it

    B. a big space in front of the window

    C. you can give it a portion of your desk

    D. just a little spot on the windowsill

5. Do you think you will remember to water your plant?

    A. You're going to try!

    B. You'll probably be good at remembering in the beginning but will forget after a while.

    C. Ya! You'll totally remember to water it.

    D. Nope.

Results!

Mostly As: Parlor Palm

This low-key plant looks like a mini palm tree! They can tolerate all sorts of light, and only a little water is needed on a regular basis.

Mostly Bs: Jade Plant

This plant, called a succulent, has small plump leaves and requires really bright light. The soil should be relatively dry, so no need to water it all the time. Unlike outdoor plants, a jade plant will bloom when the weather gets cool!

Mostly Cs: A Shamrock Plant

This plant will bring you luck! It needs partial light, regular watering, and a cool spot to hang. We have full confidence that you are up to this challenge. Just don't let your pet eat it, as it can be poisonous.

Mostly Ds: Echeveria (a pretty succulent)

You may not be the world's best gardener, but you can take care of this little plant. It has a unique flower shape and looks like something from another planet. It needs lots of sun, and it's totally cool if you forget to water it for many days.

What DIY lamp best suits your personality?

1. What do you like to do when you hang out in a park?

A. close your eyes and enjoy the sun on your face

B. make shapes out of the clouds

C. flip through a magazine

D. listen to the conversations around you

2. When you're hanging in your room, you . . .

A. listen to music

B. draw

C. paint your nails

D. dance around

3. Choose a famous pair of shoes.

A. Cinderella's glass slippers (fairy tale)

B. Hermes's winged sandals (classical mythology)

C. Dorothy's ruby slippers (*The Wizard of Oz*)

D. blue suede shoes (Elvis)

4. Pick a place to live.

A. a tree house

B. a houseboat

C. a castle

D. a decked-out camper

5. How would you like to get around?

A. flying carpet

B. giant bird

C. yacht

D. jet pack

Results!

Mostly As: String of Lights

You are all about relaxing, and your room should be as calm as you are. The soft lighting and whimsical vibe of a string of lightbulbs will set you right at ease.

What you'll need:

- You can use regular Christmas tree lights or look for ones with different-size bulbs.

Directions:

One of the easiest ways to hang lights is to use small adhesive hooks and drape the lights between them. Use clear tape to reinforce the hooks. You can also wrap the lights around bedposts or hang them from a curtain rod.

Mostly Bs: Draw Patterns on a Lightbulb

You are super creative and love dreaming up new worlds. The fantastical shadows this lightbulb casts are sure to spark your imagination.

What you'll need:

- A clear glass lightbulb and different-colored Sharpies

Directions:

Draw shapes and patterns on the lightbulb and turn the lamp on!

Mostly Cs: Cover the Inside of a Lampshade with Glitter

This glamorous lampshade will sparkle and shine, just like you do!

What you'll need:

- Glitter, Mod Podge (a heavy-duty brand of glue)

Directions:

1. Cover the inside of the shade with the Mod Podge and brush it out evenly with a paintbrush.

2. Sprinkle the glitter all over the glue and let dry.

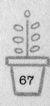

Mostly Ds: Constellation Projector

Take the stars inside by turning a jar into a constellation projector! Then you can look at the night sky from the comfort of your bed.

What you'll need:
- A clear glass jar, tinfoil, a battery-operated LED light

Directions:
1. Poke holes in the tinfoil (maybe even map out real constellations!).
2. Roll the foil into a cylinder and place it into the jar (the cylinder should be only slightly smaller than the jar).
3. Turn the light on and put it into the jar.
4. Screw on the lid and turn off the lights in your room!

How should you decorate your walls?

1. Choose something to capture an image.

    A. camera on your phone

    B. paints and canvas

    C. video camera

    D. Polaroid camera

2. What would you like to do this Saturday?

    A. hang with friends outside

    B. arts and crafts

    C. go to an amusement park

    D. No idea! You'll have to see how you feel.

3. Choose a wheel.

    A. Ferris wheel

    B. color wheel

    C. wheel of fortune

    D. bicycle wheel

4. Who would be your favorite teacher?

A. Miss Honey (*Matilda*)

B. Yoda (Star Wars)

C. Ms. Frizzle (The Magic School Bus)

D. Professor McGonagall (Harry Potter)

5. What museum would you most like to visit?

A. Art Institute of Chicago

B. MOMA (Museum of Modern Art),
in New York City

C. Museum of Science, in Boston

D. Natural History Museum, in New York City

Results!

Mostly As: A Wall of Colorfully Framed Pictures

You love hanging out with friends, so why not be surrounded by them all the time? Hang up your favorite pictures and put colorful or patterned tape around them for cool and easy frames.

What you'll need:

- Colorful, long-lasting tape. Washi tape is super durable and comes in lots of different colors and patterns, and you can find it at most craft supply stores. But you can use any kind of tape you like!

- Printed-out photos, cutouts from magazines, or any other image you find!

- Double-sided tape

Directions:

1. Print out photos in color or in black-and-white.

2. Tape the images to the wall using the double-sided tape.

3. Tape the washi tape around each image to create a frame. Experiment with different shapes and sizes!

Mostly Bs: The Melted Crayon Masterpiece

The perfect decoration for an arts-and-crafts lover such as yourself. This super-fun art project will leave you with a beautiful, unique decoration for your room!

What you'll need:

- A blank canvas of any size (available at most craft stores)
- Enough crayons to line up (point down, side by side) across the top of the canvas. Could be all the colors of the rainbow or just your favorites.
- Hot glue gun
- Blow dryer
- Newspaper

Directions:

1. Hot-glue the crayons point down, side by side along the top of the canvas. There shouldn't be any room between the crayons. You can leave the paper wrappers on.

2. After the glue is dry, lean the canvas against a wall so the canvas is at a slight angle. The crayons should be at the top of the canvas. Be sure to lay newspaper under the canvas to avoid any messes!

3. Turn the blow-dryer on full heat and blow-dry the tips of the crayons so the crayon wax melts down the canvas.

4. Melt the wax as much or as little as you like. Whatever you think looks best! When you're happy with it, let the wax dry.

5. Once everything is dry, peel the crayons off and pick out the leftover glue. Then you will have a beautiful, totally cool, and absolutely unique wall decoration!

Mostly Cs: A Confetti-Covered Wall

You are always on the go, doing a million different activities. Your wall art should be as active as you are! Put up a bunch of polka dots for a fun and colorful decoration!

What you'll need:

- Lots of different-colored paper (construction paper, poster board, whatever you have!)
- A circle to use as a stencil (trace the bottom of a can on a thick piece of paper and cut it out; use different-sized cans for different-sized circles)
- Scissors
- Double-sided tape

Directions:

1. Using the stencil (or stencils), cut out lots of circles in different colors from the colored paper.

2. Put the double-sided tape on one side of each circle and hang on the wall. Overlap some circles to make it look like confetti falling!

Mostly Ds: A Giant Chalkboard Wall

You love to create new things, so why not create a new wall every day? This giant chalkboard will allow your imagination to run wild!

What you'll need:

- Chalkboard paint
- Tape measure
- Painter's tape
- Chalk

Directions:

1. Measure how big you want the chalkboard on your wall to be and mark the dimensions with a pencil.

2. Use painter's tape to create the outline of the chalkboard.

3. Paint inside the tape with the chalkboard paint (follow specific directions on the paint can for this process).

4. Let dry and draw on it with chalk!

What kind of wind chime should you make to hang in your window?

1. What is the most peaceful image?

A. a sandy beach with clear blue water

B. an organized desk in front of an open window

C. a forest with dazzling shafts of light shining through the canopy

D. a beautiful sunset seen from the top of a Ferris wheel

2. What would you most want to collect?

A. sand from all over the world

B. postcards from the past

C. really old books

D. buttons of all different shapes, sizes, and colors

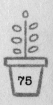

3. Choose a concert experience.

A. a group gathered around a fire with only a few instruments

B. a small room with only a handful of tables and chairs

C. lots of people in an amphitheater (an outdoor music venue) in the mountains

D. a big arena with tons of people and a crazy stage

4. When someone says "wing," you think of . . .

A. a bird

B. a plane

C. a fairy

D. the phrase "winging it"

5. Choose a cereal.

A. Frosted Flakes

B. Cinnamon Toast Crunch

C. granola

D. Froot Loops

Results!

Mostly As: Shell-and-Driftwood Wind Chime

You know how important it is to take a deep breath. This wind chime will make you feel like you're relaxing on the beach.

What you'll need:

- Seashells (available at most craft stores)
- String (different colors would be cool!)
- A stick (driftwood, if you can find it)
- Rope

Directions:

1. Tie different-length strings to different kinds of shells. You can poke holes in the shells with a nail and a hammer—just be really gentle. Or you can wrap the string around each shell and knot it securely.

2. Tie each piece of string to the stick so that the shells are spaced apart but close enough to hit one another when a breeze goes by.

3. Tie the rope to each end of the long stick, making a C shape.

4. Hang the wind chime from a nail or a hook by your window.

Mostly Bs: Pencils

The sounds of pencils gently bumping into one another will inspire you to put your own writing utensil to the page, whether it's to write a note to a friend, sketch a picture, or begin a new novel!

What you'll need:

- Ten to fifteen pencils in varying sizes and colors
- Fishing wire
- Some kind of stick

Directions:

1. Tie fishing wire to the eraser end of each pencil.

2. Hang each pencil from the larger stick, the smaller pencils toward the outside and the longer ones in the center, forming a V shape.

3. Cut a long piece of fishing wire and tie it to each end of the long stick, making a C.

4. Hang the wind chime from a nail on your window.

Mostly Cs: Painted Cans

This bright and colorful wind chime is perfectly suited for your free spirit. The colors will look great in your window (or outside it!) and will make a beautiful, unique sound.

What you'll need:

- Paint (as many colors as you want)
- Three or four cans of different sizes
- Hammer and nails
- Four-to-five-foot length of twine

Directions:

1. Paint the cans the colors you want.
2. Punch a hole through the center of the bottom of each can, using a hammer and nail.
3. Thread the twine through one can and knot the twine. Add all the cans to the twine so they overlap (it should be a string of cans, biggest at the top and smallest at the bottom).
4. Tie a rock to the end of the twine and hang it up!

Mostly Ds: Sticks

This wind chime seems like it came right out of a fairy's house. Add whimsical touches like flowers and moss to complete the look.

What you'll need:

- Five to ten sticks of different sizes
- One extra-long stick
- A thin rope

Directions:

1. Tie the rope to an end of each of the smaller sticks. Make sure to wrap the rope around the sticks a few times so it doesn't fall off. Add clear drying glue if you feel like you need the added security.

2. Tie the smaller sticks to the big stick. Make sure they're spaced apart but close enough to hit one another.

3. Tie each end of the longer piece of rope to either end of the long stick to make a V.

4. Decorate the stick with fake flowers or moss to make it really unique.

5. Hang from a nail or hook outside your window.

What is the perfect theme for you bedroom? Based on your results from the previous quizzes, what is the best look for your bedroom?

Mostly As: A Beachside Retreat (parlor palm tree, wall of frames, string of lights, shell-and-driftwood wind chime)

Make your room the perfect place to relax by pretending the beach is just outside your window.

Some more ideas:

Put fresh flowers in a vase by your bed to bring the outside in.

Place blue and green glass bottles on your windowsill.

Use a wooden chair as your bedside table. Stack books on it to make it the right height for your bed.

Mostly Bs: An Artist's Studio (jade plant, patterns on a lightbulb, melted crayon masterpiece, pencil wind chime)

Your room should be filled with things that inspire you. Whether you have a big desk or you make room on the floor, be sure to have space to create!

Some more ideas:

Put up a corkboard and pin things that make you happy, like a picture of a cool place or an inspiring quote.

Keep a journal and a pen by your bed. Write your dreams down as soon as you wake up.

Hang up posters or prints of your favorite paintings or photographs.

Mostly Cs: Colors of the Rainbow (shamrock plant, glitter lampshade, confetti-covered wall, painted-can wind chime)

Your room should be the Funfetti cake of bedrooms, an explosion of color that will make everyone smile when they walk in.

Some more ideas:

Arrange your books by color on your bookshelf, or stack them on the floor. You can even put them in rainbow order (red, orange, yellow, green, blue, purple).

Splatter-paint white pillowcases with fabric paint and an old toothbrush.

Change the drawer pulls on your dresser. You can make them all different colors and shapes.

Mostly Ds: Dreamworld (echeveria, constellation projector, giant chalkboard wall, wind chime made of sticks)

Make your room a whimsical place of dreams with ample space to sit and think.

Some more ideas:

Paint clouds on your ceiling (and make the sky a sunny blue).

Put two big pillows on top of an old trunk to make a bench.

Put a telescope in the window.

5

Cooking Discoveries

Which food group do you belong to?

What meal best describes your personality?

What fictional restaurant should you eat at?

What fictional chef are you?

What should you make for dinner?

Which food group do you belong to?

1. Choose a picture book.

   A. *Strega Nona*

   B. *The Giving Tree*

   C. *The Tale of Peter Rabbit*

   D. *If You Give a Mouse a Cookie*

2. Choose a candy.

   A. Twix bar

   B. Starbursts

   C. Reese's Peanut Butter Cups

   D. Hershey's chocolate bar

3. Choose a dip.

   A. salsa

   B. guacamole

   C. ranch

   D. nacho cheese

4. You should never leave the house without . . .

A. a snack

B. Band-Aids

C. a pair of sunglasses

D. gum

5. If you were a Disney sidekick, who would you be?

A. Olaf (*Frozen*)

B. Flounder (*The Little Mermaid*)

C. Zazu (*The Lion King*)

D. Piglet (*Winnie the Pooh*)

Results!

Mostly As: Grains

You're like bagels and pizza: you're everyone's favorite! High in dietary fiber, grains help people feel full. You always make people feel full of laughs.

Mostly Bs: Fruits

Like most fruits, you are sweet and refreshing. Fruits are high in vitamin C, which helps heal cuts and wounds. Your kind and generous spirit always makes people feel better.

Mostly Cs: Vegetables

No one can deny that you're a good influence. Vegetables are a good source of vitamin A, which helps keep eyes and skin healthy. Your honesty and straightforward attitude help people see things clearly.

Mostly Ds: Dairy

You are very cool and popular. Dairy has lots of calcium, which is great for building bones and maintaining dental health. You are a strong person, and your friends rely on your wisdom and good advice.

What meal best describes your personality?

1. Sunday mornings are for . . .

   A. taking it easy with a bowl of cereal and TV

   B. doing things! Like hanging outside or playing sports.

   C. sleeping

   D. taking your time to get ready for the day

2. Pick an ice cream flavor.

   A. mint chocolate chip

   B. chocolate

   C. vanilla

   D. strawberry

3. Pick an outfit to lounge in.

   A. jeans and sweatshirt

   B. sweatpants and a T-shirt

   C. a long cotton dress

   D. leggings and a long T-shirt

4. What would be the best part about being a witch?

A. casting spells

B. flying on a broomstick

C. making potions

D. reading the future

5. If you were a ghost, you would live . . .

A. in your attic or basement

B. Nowhere! You'd travel the world.

C. in an old abandoned mansion filled with lots of other ghosts

D. in a forest

Results!

Mostly As: Lunch

You are practical and organized. You may have a busy schedule, but you know how important it is to pause and take a minute to regroup.

Mostly Bs: Snacks

You are super busy, and you wouldn't have it any other way. You love having a million things to do—too much downtime is boring.

Mostly Cs: Dinner

You love to entertain. There's nothing more fun than planning a big party for all your friends.

Mostly Ds: Breakfast

You're always down to try something new, so you like to be prepared for everything. It's best to take the time to relax in the morning and plan for the day ahead.

What fictional restaurant should you eat at?

1. Pick a decor.

    A. neon-purple-and-green walls, rocket ships, and planets

    B. wooden tables and candlelight

    C. picnic tables outside

    D. floral wallpaper and checkered tablecloths

2. What do like to do while you wait for your food?

    A. play video games

    B. chat with your friends

    C. sit back and relax

    D. draw with crayons on the paper place mats

3. What would you like to do before dinner?

    A. lounge around in your house

    B. go shopping

    C. look at animals

    D. take in the sights

4. How would you like to get to your dinner?

    A. order it in

    B. walk down a long and winding path

    C. your car

    D. take the subway

5. What kind of atmosphere do you prefer?

    A. don't care as long as you get your food fast

    B. loud with lots of laughter and chatter

    C. a place that makes you feel like a regular

    D. quirky and weird

Results!

Mostly As: Pizza Planet (*Toy Story*)

For a casual and delicious dining experience! Play arcade games while you're waiting, or if you don't feel like going anywhere, order in!

Mostly Bs: The Three Broomsticks (Harry Potter)

You're all about relaxing and chatting with pals. Have some pub food and butterbeer at the Three Broomsticks. The cozy interior and relaxed vibe will make you feel right at ease.

Mostly Cs: Bronto Burger (The Flintstones)

This drive-in diner has been a hit since the Stone Age! You'll love the massive burgers. Plus, dinosaurs are roaming around!

Mostly Ds: Pete's Luncheonette (*The Muppets Take Manhattan*)

Pete's may not be the cleanest place in town, but it might be the funniest. Stop by to listen to Pete's employees and maybe have a chat with Kermit the Frog.

What fictional chef are you?

1. Pick a chef's outfit.

    A. big floppy hat, striped shirt, red bow tie

    B. a chef's hat and your normal clothes

    C. baseball cap, regular clothes

    D. long purple coat, top hat

2. Where would you like to live?

    A. New York City

    B. Paris

    C. in a city under the sea

    D. in a town made of candy

3. What would you like to be famous for?

    A. funny YouTube videos

    B. a cooking show

    C. starring in a television series

    D. inventing something important

4. Pick a junk food.

A. Trix cereal

B. Cheetos

C. french fries

D. Oreos

5. Choose a method of communication.

A. pigeon carriers

B. talking face-to-face

C. walkie-talkies

D. a tube that will carry a letter directly to a friend

Results!

Mostly As: Swedish Chef
(The Muppet Show)

You are outlandish and hilarious, just like the Swedish Chef from *The Muppet Show*! You may make a mess in the kitchen, but it's okay, because you always have fun doing it.

Mostly Bs: Remy (Ratatouille)

Like Remy, you have a passion for food. You have big dreams, but you'll always put your friends first, even when you're super famous.

Mostly Cs: SpongeBob

You are a ton of fun and a great friend. Everyone loves you! You never do things the way you're expected to, but things tend to work out anyway.

Mostly Ds: Willy Wonka

You've got a sweet tooth and big ideas. Your imagination knows no bounds, and everyone's always wondering what crazy-cool thing you'll come up with next.

Based on the previous questions, what should you make for dinner?

Mostly As: Pizza (grains, lunch, Pizza Planet, Swedish Chef)

Making your own pizza is easy and fun! And it's great to do with a group of people. You could even have a make-your-own-pizza party!

What you'll need:

- One bag (or box) of premade pizza dough (you can get this at most grocery stores, or look online for directions on how to make your own dough)
- One jar of marinara sauce
- Toppings for the pizzas (ideas: pepperoni, mushrooms, onions, peppers, pineapple, bacon)
- One bag of shredded mozzarella cheese

Directions:

1. Preheat the oven according to your dough's directions.

2. Roll the dough out on a large, flat pan. It doesn't have to be a circle.

3. Spread the sauce on the pizza dough.

4. Cover with shredded mozzarella.

5. Add your toppings.

6. Put the pizza in the oven (follow your dough's instructions).

7. Enjoy!

Mostly Bs: A Bunch of Snacks (fruit, snacks, the Three Broomsticks, Remy)

Decisions are hard. But there's no need to decide on one thing to eat! Just make a bunch of easy snacks!

What you'll need:

- Whatever your favorite snacks are! Some suggestions: apples and cheddar cheese, popcorn, carrots and ranch dressing, cheese and crackers, salsa and chips, celery and peanut butter, chocolate-covered pretzels, carrots and hummus.

Mostly Cs: Breaded Mozzarella Bites (vegetables, dinner, Bronto Burger, SpongeBob)

Make your home a restaurant with some restaurant-quality appetizers!

What you'll need:
- 1/3 cup bread crumbs
- 3 sticks of mozzarella string cheese
- 2 eggs
- 1/4 cup marinara sauce

Directions:
1. Preheat oven to 425°.
2. Heat olive oil in pan and pour in bread crumbs. Toast the bread crumbs for about two minutes. Set them aside in a small bowl.
3. Cut the mozzarella sticks into pieces about the size of your pinkie finger.
4. Crack the eggs in a bowl and whisk together.
5. Cover a baking sheet with tinfoil.
6. Dip each cheese piece in egg mix and then roll in the bread crumbs. Place the cheese on the baking sheet.
7. Put in the oven for three minutes.
8. Heat up the marinara sauce.
9. Dip the mozzarella pieces in the sauce!

Mostly Ds: French Toast (dairy, breakfast, Pete's Luncheonette, Willy Wonka)

An out-of-the-ordinary approach to dinner is perfect for your out-of-the-ordinary sensibility.

What you'll need:

- 1 teaspoon ground cinnamon
- 2 tablespoons sugar
- 4 tablespoons butter
- 4 eggs
- 1/4 cup milk
- 1/2 teaspoon vanilla extract
- Slices of thick white bread
- Maple syrup and fruit (optional)

Directions:

1. Whisk the cinnamon, sugar, eggs, milk, and vanilla together and pour into a shallow bowl.
2. Dip the bread into the mixture, letting it soak on each side.
3. Melt butter in a skillet.
4. Cook the soaked bread in the skillet on each side until golden brown.
5. Serve with maple syrup and fruit!

6

Space Explorations

What famous alien should be your best friend?

On which planet should you vacation?

How will you change the future of space travel?

What constellation are you?

What landmark NASA mission are you?

What famous alien should be your best friend?

1. Where do you like to hang out?

    A. your living room

    B. pizza place

    C. you like to bike around the neighborhood

    D. Who has time to just hang out?

2. What kind of friend are you?

    A. supportive

    B. funny

    C. fun

    D. loyal

3. What eyewear suits your style?

    A. a monocle

    B. sunglasses

    C. fake glasses with a nose and mustache

    D. prescription glasses

4. Choose a special ability.

   A. levitation

   B. superstrength

   C. able to change your appearance

   D. laser beam–shooting eyes

5. Which competition would you most like to win?

   A. science fair

   B. art fair

   C. talent show

   D. track meet

Results!

Mostly As: E.T.

E.T. is a good friend and supersmart. You guys could learn a lot from each other! And you would have a lot of fun on a flying bicycle.

Mostly Bs: Chewbacca (Star Wars)

You guys may not speak the same language, but you can always tell what he's thinking. He is fun and sassy, and he'll always be there for you when you need him.

Mostly Cs: Bumblebee (Transformers)

You can relate to this goofy underdog of the Transformers gang. Neither of you take things too seriously.

Mostly Ds: Superman

Superman is a pretty busy guy, so he might not be around all that much. But what he lacks in time he makes up for in fun activities, like flying around and lifting up heavy things. Think of all the fun pranks you can play together!

On which planet should you vacation?

1. What sounds like the most fun?

   A. diving for lost treasure in sunken ships

   B. watching a meteor shower on a beach

   C. spelunking in crystal caves

   D. watching a volcano erupt

2. Which job sounds like the most fun?

   A. pirate

   B. astronomer

   c. professional athlete

   d. diplomat

3. Which is *least* annoying out of the following list?

   A. getting dust in your eye

   B. superhot sand you have to walk across barefoot

   C. being hit in the back of the head unexpectedly

   D. a cold that makes it hard to breathe

4. What animal would be your space adventure sidekick?

A. a dolphin

B. a camel

C. a monkey

D. an elephant

5. Which outfit would you like to wear in space?

A. a scuba suit

B. a superhero outfit

C. a race car driver's outfit

D. your regular clothes

Results!

Mostly As: Jupiter

Dive into Jupiter's gaseous layers for Zeus's treasure!

Jupiter is a gaseous planet made up of different layers that get denser as you get closer to its rocky core. Jupiter is the Roman name for Zeus, god of the sky and ruler of Mount Olympus. Go find some space treasures as you dive among the debris of this cool planet!

Mostly Bs: Mercury

Visit Mercury for the craziest sunset you'll ever see.

Mercury is a pretty volatile planet. It's superhot, and huge storms rage across it constantly. But: it has the craziest sunset. Due to the nature of its orbit, the sun rises and becomes larger until it reaches its highest point in the sky. Then it stops, and starts going back from where it came. Then the sun stops again and goes back the way it was going in the first place. While this is happening, the stars are moving three times faster than they do on Earth.

Mostly Cs: Saturn

Dodge debris on Saturn's Rings Racetrack.

Like Saturn itself, the planet's rings are made up of gaseous material. Tons of dust and debris float within the rings. Race around Saturn's natural racetrack while dodging all the particles!

Mostly Ds: Venus

Visit Venus, Earth's sister planet! Cast your vote: Spot for human settlement or not?

Venus is often called Earth's sister planet because of its size and mass. It lacks a lot of the luxuries of Earth, though, like our oceans and nice atmosphere. It has a desertlike surface and lots of volcanoes. But some scientists believe people could live on this planet someday. Have a look for yourself! Does it seem like a fun, beautiful place to live, or is it just a place to visit once in a while?

How will you change the future of space travel?

1. Choose something from the past.

   A. the telegraph

   B. a covered wagon

   C. a suit of armor

   D. the World's Fair

2. What would you like to write on?

   A. a postcard

   B. a computer

   C. marble (so, technically, you would be etching)

   D. a chalkboard

3. Pick a backyard activity.

   A. tag

   B. jumping on the trampoline

   C. snowball fight

   D. building a fort

4. At a party you can be found . . .

A. making new friends

B. dancing

C. playing games

D. helping the host

5. What would you like to do in space?

A. land on Mars

B. go to another galaxy

C. ride a comet

D. live on the rocket ship

Results!

Mostly As: Alien Contact

You will be the first person to make contact with aliens. You are super outgoing and friendly and can make everyone feel comfortable. You will be the perfect ambassador for humans!

Mostly Bs: Travel at the Speed of Light

You will figure out how to travel at the speed of light. You're all about going new places, so exploring new galaxies is the natural next step for you.

Mostly Cs: An Indestructible Space Suit

You will develop the technology for a lightweight space suit that protects you from everything. Protecting ourselves from the unknown elements will allow us to go anywhere!

Mostly Ds: Earth's First Intergalactic Space Station

You will create the first human-run intergalactic space station. You are all about community and know that providing a safe space for people to meet will be the first step to universal peace.

What constellation are you?

1. Pick a place to look at the stars.

   A. around a campfire

   B. the beach

   C. the roof of your house

   D. the top of a mountain

2. Choose a doodle.

   A. triangles

   B. 3-D boxes

   C. stick figures

   D. swirls

3. Pick a fictional object.

   A. the harp that sings by itself from "Jack and the Beanstalk"

   B. magic carpet

   C. the Fountain of Youth

   D. Batmobile

4. How would you like good news delivered?

A. a singing telegram

B. written in the sky with a plane

C. in a complex code only the recipient will be able to figure out

D. the newspaper

5. Favorite picture book?

A. *Horton Hears a Who*

B. *The Rainbow Fish*

C. *The Giving Tree*

D. *Where the Wild Things Are*

Results!

Mostly As: Lyra, the Harp

Orpheus played the most beautiful music ever heard. His talents could even move rivers! When he died, the gods placed his harp in the sky for everyone to see. You also have amazing musical talents. You might be a singer, play an instrument, or put together really good playlists. Whatever it is, people can't wait to hear what you've come up with!

Mostly Bs: Pegasus, the Flying Horse

This miraculous horse helped people win a lot of battles, carried around Zeus's thunderbolts, and created a river by digging his hoof into the ground. Like Pegasus, you are talented and unique, and you're always there when someone needs you.

Mostly Cs: Gemini, the Twins

This constellation looks like two stick figures with their arms over each other's shoulders. In Greek mythology, they were two brothers who wanted to be together for all eternity. You're super close to your family and friends too. You hate being alone and would spend all your time hanging with pals if you could!

Mostly Ds: Auriga, the Charioteer

Zeus placed Auriga in the sky to honor his invention, the chariot! Greek mythology says that Zeus brought the four-horse chariot to Earth and modeled it after the sun god's chariot. You too will invent something that changes the world! Your creativity knows no bounds.

What landmark NASA mission are you?

1. How would you like to float down a river?

A. with a wet suit and a snorkel

B. in a raft

C. on an inner tube

D. in a kayak

2. Choose a space discovery.

A. Mars once had liquid water

B. the moon is 4.527 billion years old

C. what Earth looks like from space

D. Saturn's rings

3. How would you like to make your groundbreaking discovery about space?

A. study a live feed

B. go into space

C. interview astronauts

D. by observing through a telescope

4. What job sounds like the most fun?

A. archeologist

B. deep-sea diver

C. movie star

D. journalist

5. What Olympic event would you like to compete in?

A. bobsled

B. freestyle skiing

C. ice-skating

D. curling

Results!

Mostly As: *Spirit* and *Opportunity*

These two Mars rovers have far exceeded NASA expectations. Their mission was supposed to last only ninety days, but the rovers have continued to explore Mars since their landing in 2004. They are responsible for discovering the evidence that Mars once held liquid water. They have also been able to map a significant part of the planet's surface. Like *Spirit* and *Opportunity*, you always see things most people miss. You like to look at things from different perspectives to see the big picture.

Mostly Bs: Apollo

Apollo was the mission that put men on the moon for the very first time. And it was the first to bring celestial materials (things from space) back to Earth so we could study them. You're always impressing people with your willingness to try anything, even if it scares you a little. You are always looking for the next great adventure!

Mostly Cs: Hubble Space Telescope

Hubble is one of the better-known NASA missions. Even if you don't know what it is, chances are you've heard the name. It was able to send a telescope past Earth's atmosphere so we could see our planet from space. It also allowed for clear images of other planets, galaxies, and stars. Like Hubble, everyone tends to know your name. People can always be themselves around you because they know you'll give them a chance to show you who they really are.

Mostly Ds: *Voyager*

The *Voyager 1* and *Voyager 2* spacecraft have given us tons of information that we take for granted now. Their paths around the planets told us about Saturn's rings and Uranus's moons. *Voyager 1* is now the farthest man-made object from Earth and is transmitting information about the very edges of our solar system. Like the Voyager ships, you're always learning new things. You love to research different stuff and find out new facts!

7

Spectacular Sports

Which ancient sport would you
bring back into popularity?

What international sporting event are you?

Which sports curse could you have broken?

In which Olympic sport would you
take home the gold?

What fictional sport should you play?

Which ancient sport would you bring back into popularity?

1. Choose a ball.

    A. soccer ball

    B. bowling ball

    C. basketball

    D. having a ball

2. Choose a field.

    A. stone courtyard

    B. grassy knoll

    C. field

    D. stadium

3. How many players would you like to have on your team?

    A. seven

    B. one hundred

    C. however many want to play

    D. one

4. What do you play for?

    A. the love of the game

    B. fun

    C. glory

    D. money

5. Who's watching?

    A. royalty

    B. anyone who's around

    C. anyone who wants to play

    D. everyone in the country

Results!

Mostly As: Cuju

A very early version of soccer developed in China during the Han dynasty, cuju was played with a feather-stuffed leather ball, and the field had six crescent-shaped goals on each end. The teams were originally made up of soldiers and, later on, the noble elite. Cuju is as fun to watch as it is to play. With your natural charisma and talent on the field, you will have people flocking to play cuju with you!

Mostly Bs: Chunkey

This Native American throwing game originated in the Cahokia territory, near modern-day Missouri. It is played by rolling a flat disk called a chunkey stone. Then, while the disk is still moving, you throw a spear to where you think the chunkey stone will stop. This game doesn't just require strength and skill—you'll also need to think critically and make split-second decisions. Perfect for a thinker such as yourself!

Mostly Cs: Duck on a Rock

This medieval game is the basis for basketball, but Duck on a Rock will be even better because you can play it without any special equipment. A pile of rocks is all you need! Put one rock on top of a bigger rock, then throw another rock to knock the smaller one off the stack. Your go-with-the-flow, laid-back attitude is perfect for this game—because you can play it anywhere and you don't have to plan ahead!

Mostly Ds: Chariot Racing

This was one of the most popular of the ancient Greek and Roman Olympic games. Each chariot was driven by one man and pulled by four horses. Women weren't allowed to race back then, but this can be changed in the game's reincarnation! The chariots would race around a giant stadium called a hippodrome. Racing in such a small space could be dangerous, but it was also very lucrative. Gaius Appuleius Diocles became one of the richest men in Rome because of all the races he won!

What international sporting event are you?

1. What would you like to eat at the next game you attend?

A. nachos

B. pizza

C. popcorn

D. hot dogs

2. Favorite way to watch sports?

A. on TV, with a bunch of people

B. on TV, with one or two other people

C. in person, surrounded by friends and family

D. in person, surrounded by loud strangers

3. If you invented a sport, what would you like people to wear to the event?

A. casual clothes that represent their favorite team

B. pajamas

C. super-fancy outfits with over-the-top accessories

D. what they wear every day

4. If you worked in sports, what would your job be?

A. you'd be a player

B. you'd be an announcer

C. you'd own a team

D. you would be a mascot

5. If you could only wear one pair of shoes for the rest of your life, what kind of shoe would you chose?

A. running sneaker

B. boot

C. wedge

D. casual sneaker

Results!

Mostly As: The World Cup

You love the social aspects of watching sports. Hanging with friends and cheering loudly is the best part of being a sports fan, and you're not afraid to show your support for your team. You are the event that everyone looks forward to! Just like the World Cup, you bring people together.

Mostly Bs: The Winter Olympics

As much as you like watching sports with others, sometimes it's best when you can just sit back and relax, without all the socializing. Life is crazy busy, so you cherish the time you get by yourself. You are the Winter Olympics, the perfect thing to put on while hanging out on the couch on a cold afternoon. Just add hot chocolate to complete the scene!

Mostly Cs: Kentucky Derby

You love traditions and you love glamour. You are the Kentucky Derby. It's a sporting event where everyone wears big fancy hats and cheers loudly as the horses race by. It's the perfect blend of sophistication and fun, just like you!

Mostly Ds: Baseball World Series

Baseball games are a great place to get loud and boisterous. And the games are long, so you really get to know your neighbors. You love getting to know new people and having an excuse to yell at the top of your lungs, which is why you are the Baseball World Series. You always encourage people to let loose and be their craziest selves.

Which sports curse could you have broken?

1. Which is the worst scenario?

A. being made to move far away from your friends

B. being forced to go home from school because you smell bad

C. being hexed so that you burp frogs every Monday, all day

D. being expelled for cheating on a test

2. Who would you like to have lunch with?

A. Paul Revere

B. Hillary Clinton

C. Liam Hemsworth

D. Tom Brady

3. What do you like to do after school?

A. play sports

B. play with your pet

C. read

D. play video games

4. What city would you like to live in?

A. Boston

B. Chicago

C. Sydney

D. you'd live on a train that travels to all the US cities

5. What's the best part of being famous?

A. having fans

B. getting to go to fancy parties

C. getting stuff for free

D. being on the cover of magazines

Results!

Mostly As: The Curse of the Bambino

This is the curse that created the rivalry between the Boston Red Sox and the New York Yankees. It all started when the Red Sox sold Babe Ruth (also called the Great Bambino) to the Yankees. After the sale, it would be eighty-six years until the Red Sox won another World Series. This curse is a huge part of Boston's legacy, and you are all about hometown pride. You love where you're from and would challenge anyone who has a bad word to say about your place. You're like the spirit of Boston, which makes you qualified to have broken the Curse of the Bambino.

Mostly Bs: Curse of the Billy Goat

Billy Sianis, a local tavern owner, placed this curse on the Chicago Cubs in 1945 after he and his goat were kicked out of a Cubs game because the goat smelled so bad. The Cubs haven't won a World Series since, which means you can still break this curse! Like Billy, you never approach anything in the usual way. What's the fun in that? You might be known for having a crazy pet, wearing strange outfits all the time, or spouting weird facts if a conversation gets boring. Whatever it is, you would never allow anyone to call you normal. It is your unique and wonderful wackiness that will allow you to break the Curse of the Billy Goat.

Mostly Cs: The Curse of the Socceroos' Witch Doctor

The curse comes from the Australian national soccer team, the Socceroos. It all happened when they went to a witch doctor in 1970 before a World Cup game. The witch doctor cursed the opposing team, and the Socceroos won the game. But the team was unable to pay the witch doctor, so the witch doctor cursed *them*. The Socceroos wouldn't qualify for the World Cup again until 2006. You know that magic is real. The full moon totally affects people's moods, and ghosts definitely live in your attic. For believing in the power of witchcraft, you could have broken the Curse of the Socceroos' Witch Doctor.

Mostly Ds: The Madden Curse

The Madden Curse is the theory that any athlete featured on the Madden NFL video game series will be cursed with an injury or will play badly that season. You know that being in the spotlight isn't always easy. It might seem like all fun and games to be adored, but it's hard work! Not everyone is always going to love you, but the show must always go on. You love being the star of the show (whatever kind of show it is), and you know that it's more important to believe in yourself than to let other people define you. Your confidence and perseverance make you able to defy the Madden Curse!

In which Olympic sport would you take home the gold?

1. Choose a Roald Dahl book.

A. *Matilda*

B. *James and the Giant Peach*

C. *Charlie and the Chocolate Factory*

D. *The Witches*

2. You are given a group project. You . . .

A. set up a group meeting and send out a detailed agenda

B. divide the work evenly among everyone

C. let someone else take the lead but do your part

D. do the project yourself—that way it'll get done

3. Favorite piece of sports gear?

A. knee pads

B. goggles

C. helmet

D. jersey

4. If you were an elf and lived in a tree, what kind of tree would you live in?

A. oak tree

B. palm tree

C. evergreen

D. weeping willow

5. Pick a Disney movie.

A. *Tangled*

B. *Finding Nemo*

C. *Toy Story*

D. *Frozen*

Results!

Mostly As: Gymnastics

You will win the gold for your fantastic floor routine in the gymnastics category. You have a flair for the dramatic, and this is the perfect place for you to shine. The crowd will go wild for your originality and heart!

Mostly Bs: Swimming

Whether you win the gold for your perfect dive or for the fastest time, you will dominate in the water. You are calm and levelheaded. It takes a lot for you to lose focus.

Mostly Cs: Skiing

You are an adrenaline junkie: you love the thrill of the wind in your face as you bomb down a mountain. Whether you're soaring into the air or dodging poles, your daring personality thrives on excitement.

Mostly Ds: Figure Skating

You love all things that sparkle. There is nothing better than floating on the ice and jumping into the air. You always have a big smile on your face, and your positive attitude makes other people smile in return!

What fictional sport should you play?

1. Choose a fictional team to play on.

    A. the Mighty Ducks (*The Mighty Ducks*)

    B. the Tune Squad (*Space Jam*)

    C. Bedrock Boulders (*The Flintstones*)

    D. the Sandlot team (*The Sandlot*)

2. What would your magical power be?

    A. flying

    B. can shrink really small

    C. superspeed

    D. can talk to animals

3. Pick a pattern.

    A. stripes

    B. checkerboard

    C. squiggly lines

    D. tiger stripes

4. Who has the best style?

   A. Waldo (Where's Waldo?)

   B. Cinderella

   C. Buzz Lightyear

   D. Charlie Brown

5. Pick a real-life sport.

   A. basketball

   B. field hockey

   C. track

   D. lacrosse

Results!

Mostly As: Quidditch (Harry Potter)

You should be flying around on a broomstick and scoring goals! You love the thrill of adventure and wish your classes were all about magic. Your curious spirit would fit right into the famous school for witchcraft and wizardry, but it's also appreciated here in the Muggle world. People always want to hang with you because you're so much fun. Life is never boring when you're around—you're always full of such great ideas.

Mostly Bs: Croquet Using Flamingos as Mallets *(Alice's Adventures in Wonderland)*

You see the world in a totally different way than everyone else, and that's awesome. Being odd can be a lot more interesting than being normal. After all, Alice had quite a bit of fun on her weird adventures in Wonderland. Play croquet with plastic flamingos—it'll still be fun, and you won't be harming any innocent animals.

Mostly Cs: Pod Racing (*Star Wars Episode I: The Phantom Menace*)

You're looking forward to the future because of all the awesome gadgets coming your way. But nothing is more exciting that the possibility of hovercrafts . . . or maybe robots? Or jet packs? Hard to decide. The future is going to be great. You will be pod racing better than Anakin Skywalker as soon as the option becomes available.

Mostly Ds: Calvinball (*Calvin and Hobbes*)

The Calvinball rules are: you must wear a mask, you can make a new rule at any time, you can use the Calvinball however you want, and penalties come in the form of embarrassment. This is the perfect game for your restless spirit. There is nothing worse for you than having to do the same thing over and over. You love adventure and trying new things.

8

All About the Animals

What creature that is now believed to be
mythical will you discover?

If you were a mermaid who lived
under the sea, what kind of animal would
be your sea creature sidekick?

What famous cartoon pet are you?

What job involving animals
would be perfect for you?

What's your spirit animal?

What creature that is now believed to be mythical will you discover?

1. What are you most likely to get in trouble for at the dinner table?

A. sitting in your chair incorrectly

B. blowing bubbles in your drink

C. talking with food in your mouth

D. making masterpieces with your food

2. If you were to go on an epic quest, what would you bring with you?

A. extra pair of boots

B. a net

C. map

D. sword

3. What kind of pet do you want?

A. dog

B. fish

C. eh, don't really want a pet

D. pony

4. What kind of reporter would you want to be?

A. science and nature writer

B. TV news reporter

C. journalist at a newspaper

D. documentary filmmaker

5. What kind of book are you most likely to read over vacation?

A. classic

B. fantasy

C. comic books

D. history

Results!

Mostly As: Sasquatch

You love all things outdoors! Hiking and camping are favorite activities of yours, so it would be easy to get along with these forest dwellers. They might be big and hairy and a little scary, but you always find a way to relate to everyone, and the Sasquatch will be no different!

Mostly Bs: Loch Ness Monster

You could spend all your time in the water. One day, you'll be swimming along and happen upon this famous creature. You guys will be the best of friends and travel the world in one giant underwater adventure.

Mostly Cs: Elf

You love to chat, so you would get along very well with an elf. An elf could trust you with any secret— that's just the kind of friend you are.

Mostly Ds: Unicorn

It would be so cool to meet a unicorn! So many things to find out. Does it sparkle? What does it smell like? Does it talk? You are very fair and kind and would not get overexcited trying to learn these things and scare it off. You have a heart of gold and would be sure to protect this animal from people who might try to harm it.

If you were a mermaid who lived under the sea, what kind of animal would be your sea creature sidekick?

1. What would be your favorite underwater activity?

   A. playing in the Coral Reef Conch Shell Band

   B. sea horse racing

   C. sunken ship treasure hunting

   D. playing tricks on fishermen

2. What would you miss most about being human?

   A. watching TV

   B. hiking, biking, and skiing down mountains

   C. watching the sunset

   D. dancing (it's not the same without feet)

3. Where would your underwater home be?

  A. a house made of pebbles and sea-glass windows

  B. No home! You'd just travel the open waters.

  C. sunken cruise ship

  D. the coral reef

4. How would you get your news of the outside world?

  A. find newspapers on the beach and read them on your favorite rock

  B. listen to the radio that plays on the ships

  C. talk to the seagulls

  D. ocean gossip

5. Pick a song.

  A. "Octopus's Garden" (The Beatles)

  B. "Under the Sea" (*The Little Mermaid*)

  C. "(Sittin' on) the Dock of the Bay" (Otis Redding)

  D. "Surfin' USA" (The Beach Boys)

Results!

Mostly As: Octopus

You are kind of a homebody. You love to relax, listen to music, and enjoy the space you're in. This eight-legged friend will be the perfect companion for your chill travels on the ocean floor.

Mostly Bs: Whale

You can't wait to see the world. You want to go everywhere and see everything. A whale would be the perfect partner to explore all the oceans with you. Plus, you could totally rest your tail and lie on a whale's back when you get tired.

Mostly Cs: Clown Fish

You could go anywhere with this little guy. You have a curious nature, so you're always asking questions and wondering about how things work. You guys could even be underwater detectives together.

Mostly Ds: Dolphins

These beautiful creatures are super social, just like you! You love to be in big groups of people, laughing and chatting. You guys would be the life of any party.

What famous cartoon pet are you?

1. Favorite food?

    A. lasagna

    B. You love all food and could never choose just one thing.

    C. burgers

    D. bananas

2. How would you like to get some exercise?

    A. Ugh. No thank you.

    B. dancing

    C. walking around

    D. gymnastics

3. Which famous person would you most like to meet?

    A. Julia Child

    B. J. K. Rowling

    C. Albert Einstein

    D. Harry Houdini

4. What do you get in trouble for in class?

A. falling asleep

B. daydreaming and not paying attention

C. nothing—you're always on your best behavior

D. pranking people

5. Pick a signature print.

A. leopard print

B. black-and-white polka dots

C. neon swirl patterns

D. bright purple everything

Results!

Mostly As: Garfield *(Garfield)*

Garfield may be the laziest cartoon cat, but he is also the funniest. You both have a quick wit and a great sense of humor. You always make everyone laugh. You're a great friend on any occasion, but you prefer the ones where food is involved.

Mostly Bs: Snoopy *(Peanuts)*

This happy dog loves to spend his time daydreaming. You both love to think about where life could take you. You have tons of great ideas and big plans for the future.

Mostly Cs: Gary the Snail (*SpongeBob SquarePants*)

Gary might be the smartest creature in Bikini Bottom. So what if he doesn't talk? He reads everything and always has great advice. Just like Gary, you are humble and wise. Your friends always look to you for advice, and they know you are always levelheaded when giving it.

Mostly Ds: Abu (*Aladdin*)

Aladdin wouldn't be able to get by without his best pal, Abu. Like Abu, you always cheer your friends up when they're feeling down. Your just make people feel better. You're always telling jokes and playing pranks, and everything is more fun when you're around!

What job involving animals would be perfect for you?

1. Pick a movie.

   A. *Jurassic Park*

   B. *We Bought a Zoo*

   C. *Dr. Doolittle*

   D. *Babe*

2. Best way to hang with animals?

   A. on a farm

   B. pet sitting

   C. snorkeling

   D. being a dog walker

3. Pick a subject in school.

   A. history

   B. English

   C. science

   D. gym

4. Pick an organization to work for.

A. Wild Animal Sanctuary

B. ASCPA (American Society for the Prevention of Cruelty to Animals)

C. World Vets

D. Guide Dog Foundation

5. Pick a type of book.

A. field guide

B. journal

C. encyclopedia

D. almanac

Results!

Mostly As: Zoologist

You like to figure out how things work. You'll love studying animals in their natural habitats and learning all the things animals have to teach us.

Mostly Bs: Shelter Owner

You would love to live with tons of animals all the time, but that's just not very practical. *Unless* you have a shelter! You'll love being surrounded by pets and making sure they all find good homes.

Mostly Cs: Vet

Your caring nature and love of science would make you a great vet. You wish you could help all the animals in need, and opening up a veterinary clinic would be a great start.

Mostly Ds: Trainer

You love the stage! So of course your pets will too. You can train them for stardom or just to impress the neighbors with your pets' good behavior.

What's your spirit animal?

1. Best part of summer?
   A. the beach
   B. Slip 'N Slide
   C. amusement parks
   D. Ugh! Summer is the worst.

2. Choose an outfit.
   A. patterned dress
   B. overalls
   C. sweat suit
   D. tuxedo

3. Choose a living situation.
   A. tent
   B. train
   C. tree house
   D. igloo

4. Pick a color.

    A. orange

    B. gray

    C. green

    D. purple

5. Choose a magical ability.

    A. can go for weeks without food or water

    B. photographic memory

    C. superstrength

    D. can breathe underwater

Results!

Mostly As: Camel

You love to travel and take long walks. You tend to go with the flow, and you don't need too much to be happy.

Mostly Bs: Elephant

You are friendly, kind, and very social. You are happiest when you are surrounded by friends and family.

Mostly Cs: Bear

You love to hibernate with TV marathons in the winter and want to be outdoors all summer long. You're all about the balance between fun and relaxation.

Mostly Ds: Penguin

You love being in a sea of people, from outdoor concerts to big cities. Wherever you are, you always look spiffy!

CHAPTER 9

World Travel

In what vehicle should you
travel the world?

Which famous traveler are you?

What kind of vacation should you go on?

In what book should you vacation?

What's the reason for
your world travels?

In what vehicle should you travel the world?

1. What animal would you most like to be?

A. whale

B. lion

C. bird

D. dog

2. If you were stranded on a desert island, which would be the most important to have?

A. fishing pole

B. jacket

C. matches

D. map of the island

3. Which is the best movie?

A. *Finding Nemo*

B. *Wreck-It Ralph*

C. *Aladdin*

D. *Mary Poppins*

4. What would you like to see in the United States?

A. Niagara Falls

B. the Grand Canyon

C. Big Sur

D. crop circles

5. Which type of vacation sounds best?

A. island vacation

B. road trip

C. hot-air balloon rides

D. backpacking through different cities

Results!

Mostly As: Sailboat

You feel most at home by the sea. You love the calm, relaxing vibe of the ocean air. This mode of transport will take you where the wind blows, but you can always dock if you want to explore.

Mostly Bs: Convertible

You're all about the getting there, not the destination. You will love zooming through the countryside, the top down and the wind in your hair. No need for a plan with this transportation; you can just stop wherever you like. Perfect for your go-with-the-flow and sometimes indecisive personality.

Mostly Cs: Helicopter

Perfect for your glamorous life style. You are always ready for a new adventure, so obviously, you need to have a vehicle that can go anywhere!

Mostly Ds: A Magical Ticket That Gets into Any Public Transportation

Wherever you go, you like to try to live like a local. You want to get the feel of the city as if you've known it forever, even if you'll be there only a couple of days. A magical transit ticket would be the perfect way for you to see everything a place has to offer.

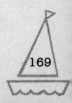

Which famous traveler are you?

1. What would you like to hang or put on your ceiling?

    A. origami birds

    B. glow-in-the-dark stars

    C. a giant map

    D. Christmas lights crisscrossed in a pattern

2. Favorite thing to do at a carnival?

    A. roller coaster

    B. Ferris wheel

    C. tarot card reader

    D. dunk tank

3. Pick a bag.

    A. rolling suitcase

    B. backpack

    C. No bag!

    D. leather suitcase

4. What's your favorite thing about school?

A. science experiments

B. all the different subjects

C. writing

D. hanging with your friends all day

5. Choose a career.

A. pilot

B. astronaut

C. reporter

D. stunt double

Results!

Mostly As: Amelia Earhart

Born in 1897, Amelia Earhart is still famous today for her achievements in the air and on the road. She was the first woman to fly solo across the Atlantic Ocean, she wrote bestselling books about her experiences flying, and she was instrumental in creating the Ninety-Nines, an organization for female pilots. Not only did Amelia break boundaries, she also made it possible for others to continue in her footsteps. Like Amelia, you know how important it is to help others!

Mostly Bs: Sally Ride

Sally was the youngest American and the first American woman to go into space. Ride wasn't just interested in science, though. She graduated from college with degrees in English as well as physics and was even training to become a professional tennis player before deciding to attend graduate school to study science. Like Sally, you are interested in a bunch of different things. Having many interests is what makes you, you.

Mostly Cs: Annie Edson Taylor

On her sixty-third birthday, in 1901, Annie Edson Taylor became the first person to survive a trip over Niagara Falls in a barrel. Annie designed a custom-made barrel for the trip. It was made of oak and steel and had a mattress inside. Like Annie, you are anything but conventional. You love to tell a good story and make people laugh.

Mostly Ds: Nellie Bly

Nellie Bly was a famous American journalist. Her investigations were groundbreaking because she wouldn't just interview people—she would go under-cover to find out the real story. One of her inves-tigations resulted in a series of articles about the terrible conditions in an insane asylum, later pub-lished as a book called *Ten Days in a Mad-House*. To research the story, she pretended to be insane in order to be sent to the Blackwell's Island Lunatic Asylum in New York City. Her work exposed the lack of funding and poor treatment of patients. Like Nellie, you are unafraid of the unknown and confi-dent in your ability to meet any challenge.

What kind of vacation should you go on?

1. Pick a way to get down the street.

   A. Rollerblades

   B. scooter

   C. moon shoes

   D. pogo stick

2. Favorite drink?

   A. ginger ale

   B. lemonade

   C. orange juice

   D. hot cocoa

3. Dream job?

   A. writer

   B. astronaut

   C. circus performer

   D. Olympic athlete

4. If you had to carry one thing around with you forever, what would you choose?

A. umbrella

B. water gun

C. jump rope

D. Polaroid camera

5. Which mythical creatures would you like to have living next door?

A. gnomes

B. mermaids

C. leprechauns

D. Sasquatches

Results!

Mostly As: Safari

See the animals you've read about in their natural habitat! You love an adventure, and this would be the trip of lifetime.

Mostly Bs: Deep-Sea Dive

Some people say that the ocean floor is the next great frontier. One dive down there will have you thinking they're on to something. You'll get to see so many crazy creatures you never even knew existed!

Mostly Cs: Tree House Forest

It's like something out of a dream. A big beautiful forest full of interconnected tree houses. Can you imagine watching the sunset through a canopy of beautiful green leaves?

Mostly Ds: Winter Mountains

Ski, snowboard, or sled down a mountain at top speed! Snowshoe to the top of a mountain to watch the sunset! Hang out on a cozy couch by the fire! There are so many options for fun—you'll never get bored up there in the mountains.

In what book should you vacation?

1. Animal sidekick?

  A. a friendly fish

  B. a cute mouse in clothes

  C. a dog

  D. a penguin

2. What city would you like to live in?

  A. Chicago

  B. London

  C. You wouldn't live in a city.

  D. Moscow

3. Pick a way to get around.

  A. sailboat

  B. Rollerblades

  C. a horse

  D. train

177

4. Where would you like to live?

A. on a cruise ship

B. in a cozy house

C. in a tree fort

D. a kingdom in the winter

5. What would you like to be for Halloween?

A. pirate

B. Amelia Earhart

C. monster

D. elf

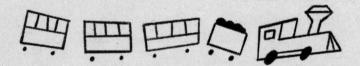

Results!

Mostly As: *The True Confessions of Charlotte Doyle* by Avi

In this classic novel, we see a young girl go from a proper lady to an unconventional pirate. Hop along on this seafaring adventure with one awesome heroine.

Mostly Bs: *The Borrowers* by Mary Norton

You're kind of a homebody, so why not stay in a cozy house for your vacation? You'll just be miniature size! You'll get such a different perspective on life.

Mostly Cs: *Where the Wild Things Are* by Maurice Sendak

Travel around with some crazy-cool monsters in a beautiful forest! You aren't afraid of anything, so you'll fit right in.

Mostly Ds: *The Polar Express* by Chris Van Allsburg

You love the cold and you love new places, so Santa's village will be the perfect destination to explore.

What's the reason for your world travels?

1. Which board game would you like to play?

A. Guess Who?

B. Operation

C. Monopoly

D. Apples to Apples

2. Which famous character would you play in a movie?

A. Sherlock Holmes

B. Dr. Frankenstein

C. Aladdin

D. Dorothy from *The Wizard of Oz*

3. What's the most important thing to bring with you on vacation?

A. a book about the place you're visiting

B. a first aid kit

C. an empty bag to bring back all the stuff you find

D. an open mind

4. What's your dream travel outfit?

A. a long trench coat and a cool hat

B. an important-looking vest with lots of pockets

C. a fancy suit

D. depends on where you're going

5. Pick a way to see things.

A. through sunglasses

B. through binoculars

C. through a monocle

D. through a cool pair of glasses

Results!

Mostly As: You Are a Spy

You are savvy and smart, and you know how to be subtle about things. Your quick wit and resourcefulness will save the world time and again . . . though we may never know your name.

Mostly Bs: You Are a Doctor Without Borders

You are caring, kind, and extremely smart. Your great energy will heal the world.

Mostly Cs: You Run an International Business

You've got lots of great ideas and a head for finance. You will be jetting around the world for your very cool business. It goes without saying that your business will be socially and environmentally responsible!

Mostly Ds: You Are a Diplomat

You are calm and kind. You always listen to others and try to understand where everyone is coming from. Your fair and calm personality will negotiate world peace someday!

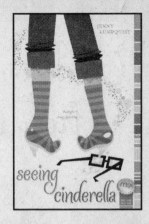

Check out these great titles from Aladdin M!X: